CONTENTS

Half-Breeds

A creature from Greek mythology, the centaur has the upper body of a human joined onto the legs and trunk of a horse. Powerful, swift, and wild, the legendary centaur is usually a danger to humans and itself.

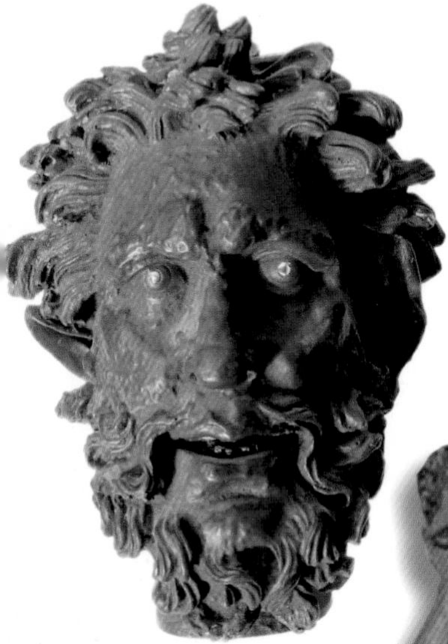

In ancient art, centaurs were often shown with horns, pointed ears, and hairy upper bodies.

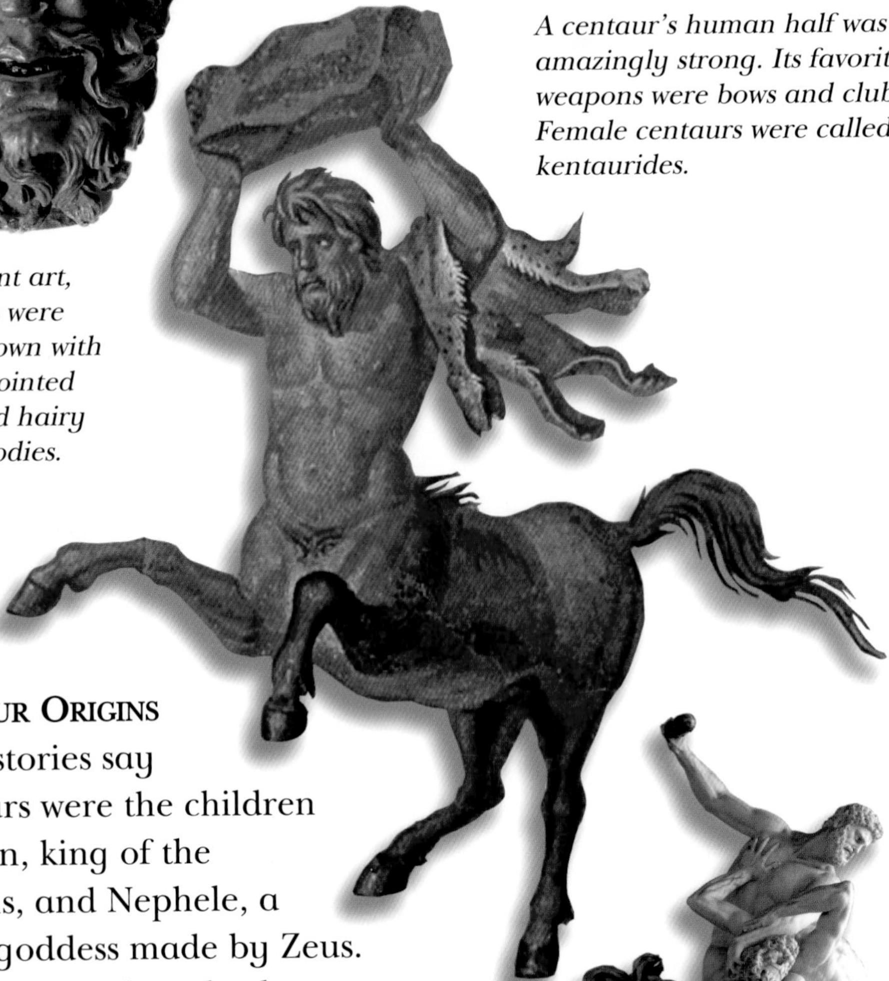

A centaur's human half was amazingly strong. Its favorite weapons were bows and clubs. Female centaurs were called kentaurides.

Centaur Origins

Some stories say centaurs were the children of Ixion, king of the Lapiths, and Nephele, a cloud goddess made by Zeus. The ancients thought the centaurs lived in Thessaly, on the slopes of Mount Pelion in northern Greece.

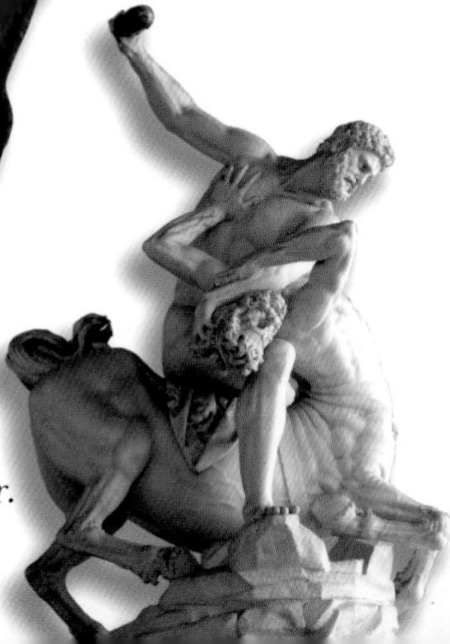

A Greek hero defeats a centaur.

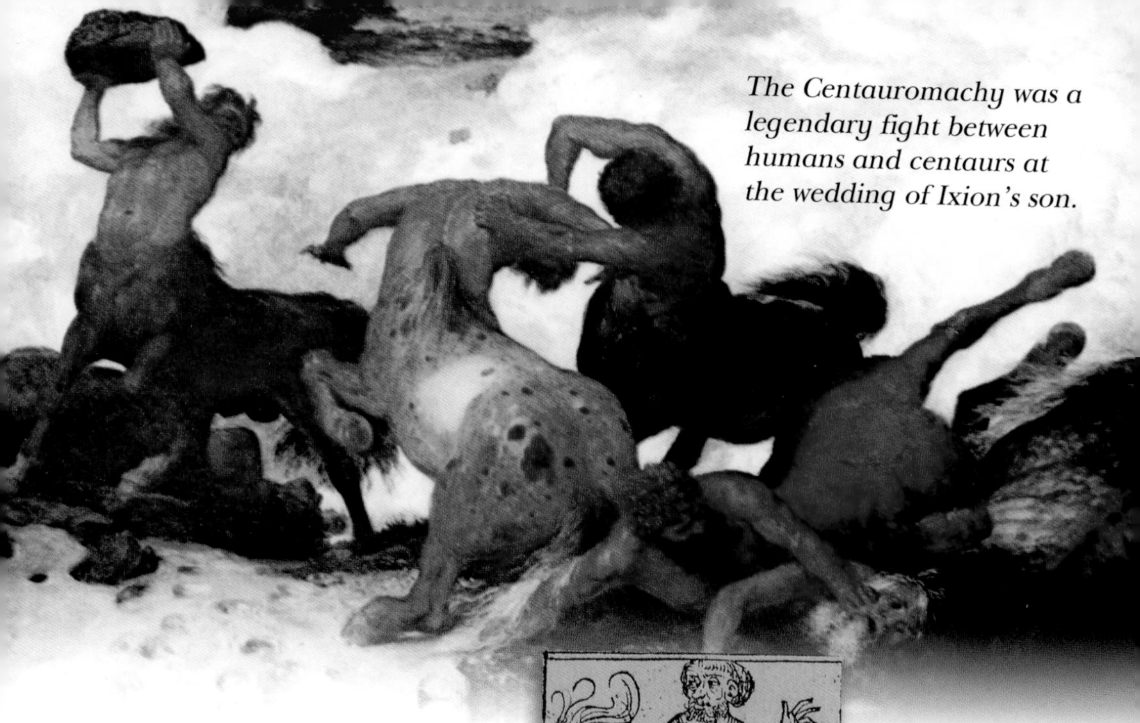

The Centauromachy was a legendary fight between humans and centaurs at the wedding of Ixion's son.

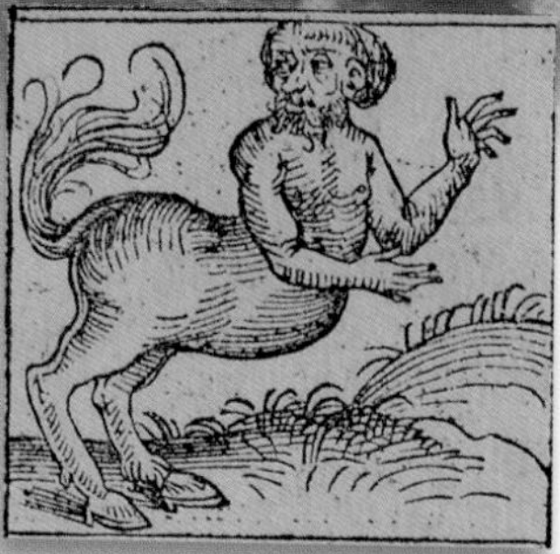

A 15th-century drawing of an ipotane—a man's body on a horse's back legs.

CENTAUR HABITS

As with many other half-human creatures, the animal side of centaurs usually won out. They loved to fight and were always on the lookout for raw flesh—their favorite food. Centaurs loved to revel, and they worshipped Dionysus, the god of wine.

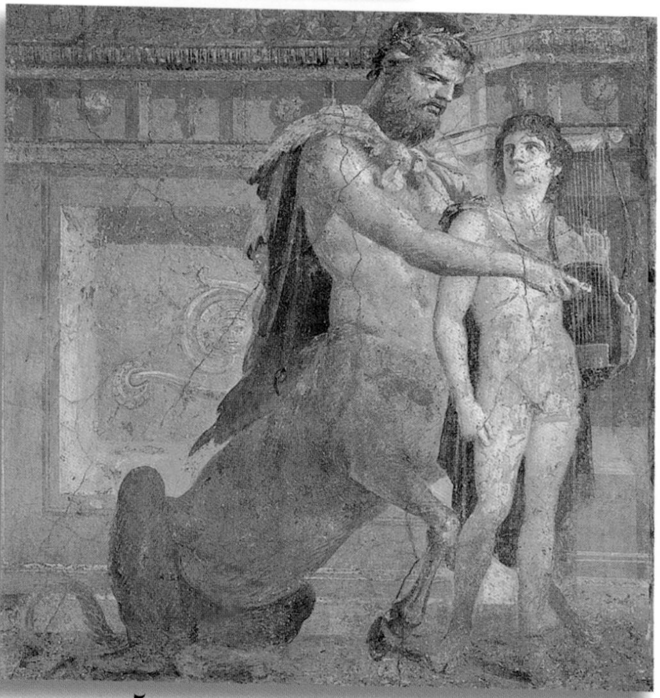

Not all centaurs were troublesome. Chiron was well educated and gentle. He became famous as the tutor of Achilles, hero of Troy. He was also a great friend to Hercules.

HERCULES AND THE CENTAURS

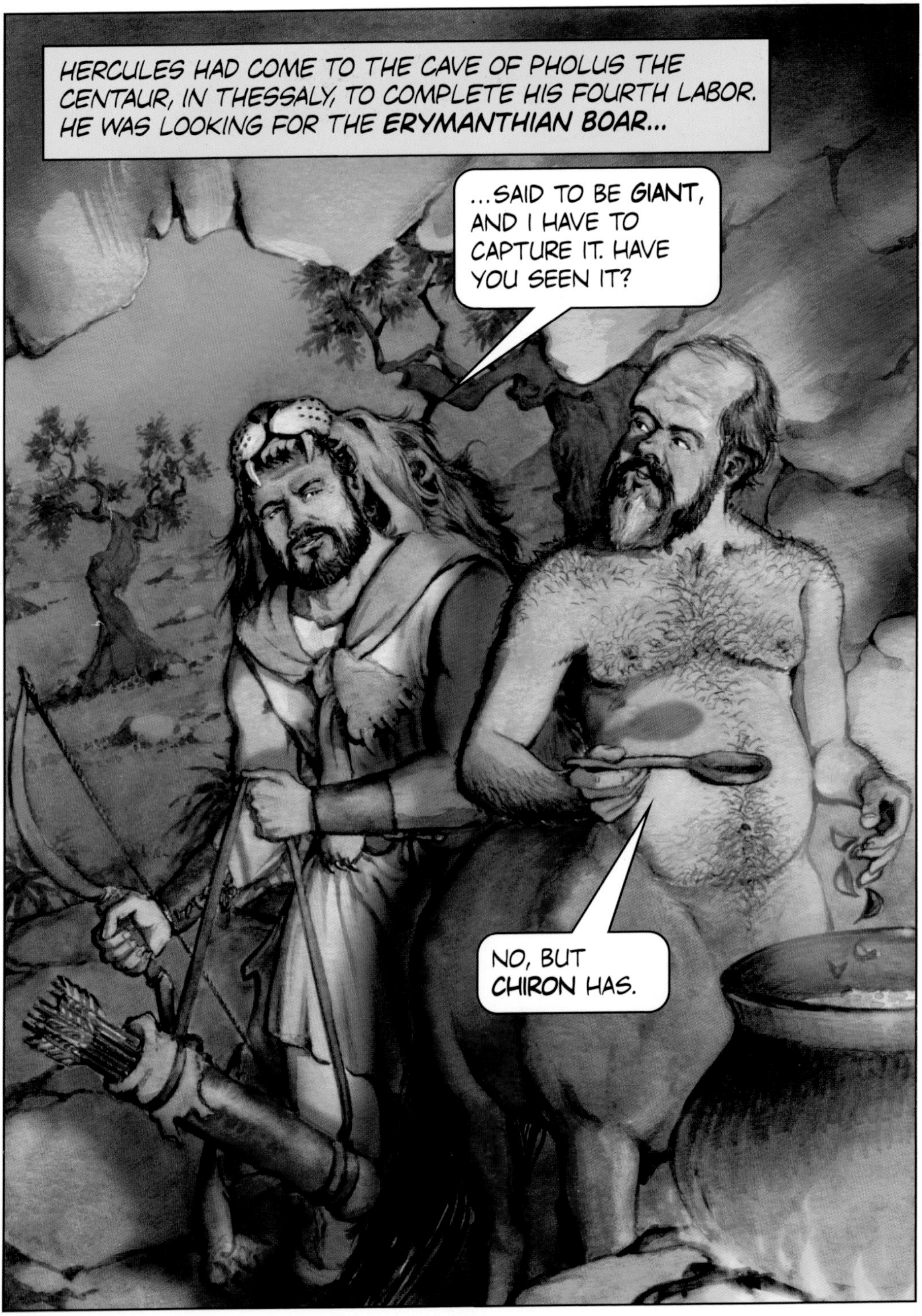

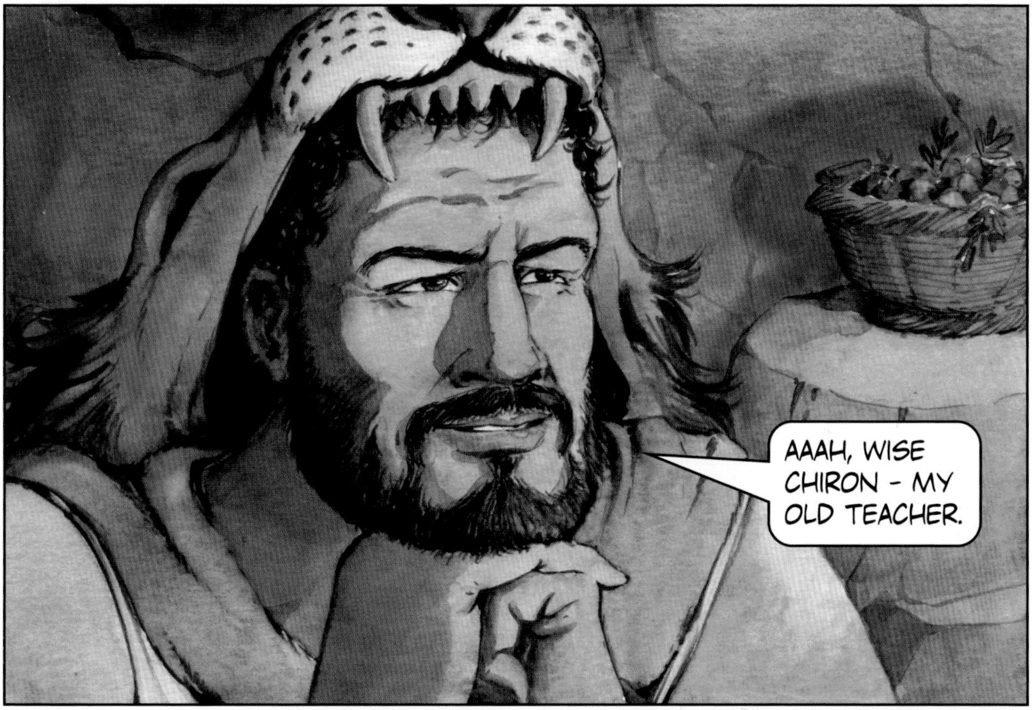
AAAH, WISE CHIRON - MY OLD TEACHER.

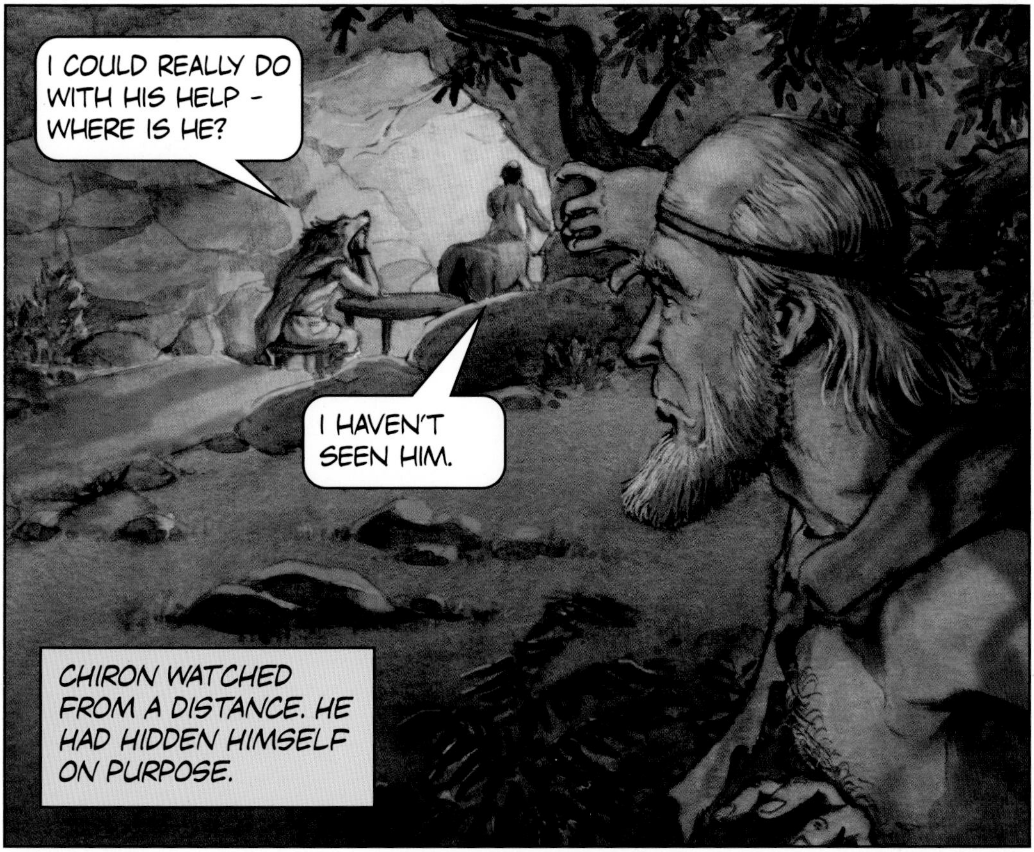
I COULD REALLY DO WITH HIS HELP - WHERE IS HE?
I HAVEN'T SEEN HIM.
CHIRON WATCHED FROM A DISTANCE. HE HAD HIDDEN HIMSELF ON PURPOSE.

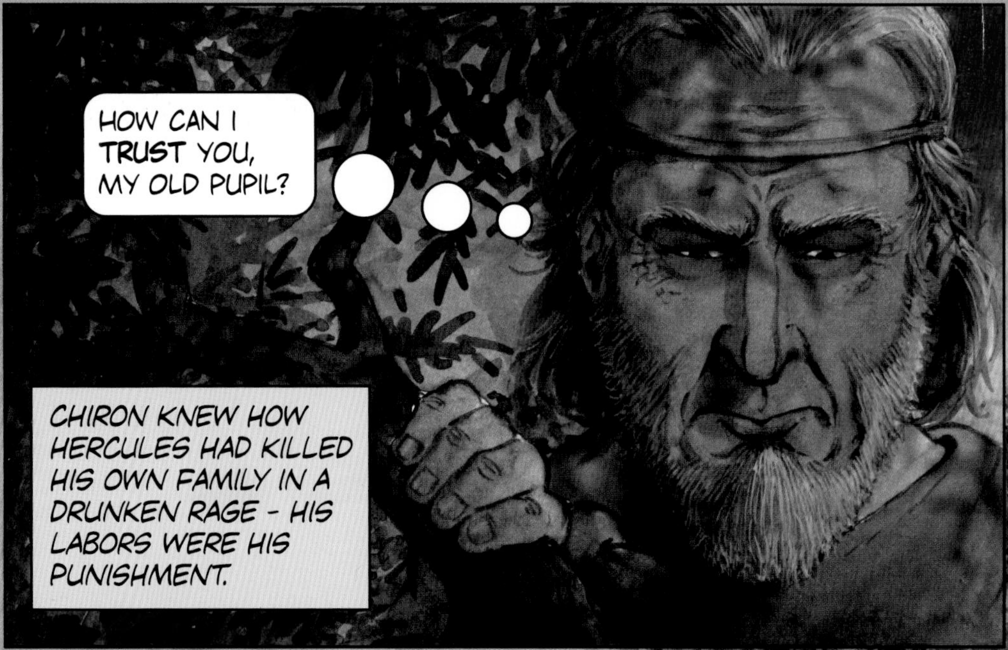
HOW CAN I TRUST YOU, MY OLD PUPIL?
CHIRON KNEW HOW HERCULES HAD KILLED HIS OWN FAMILY IN A DRUNKEN RAGE - HIS LABORS WERE HIS PUNISHMENT.

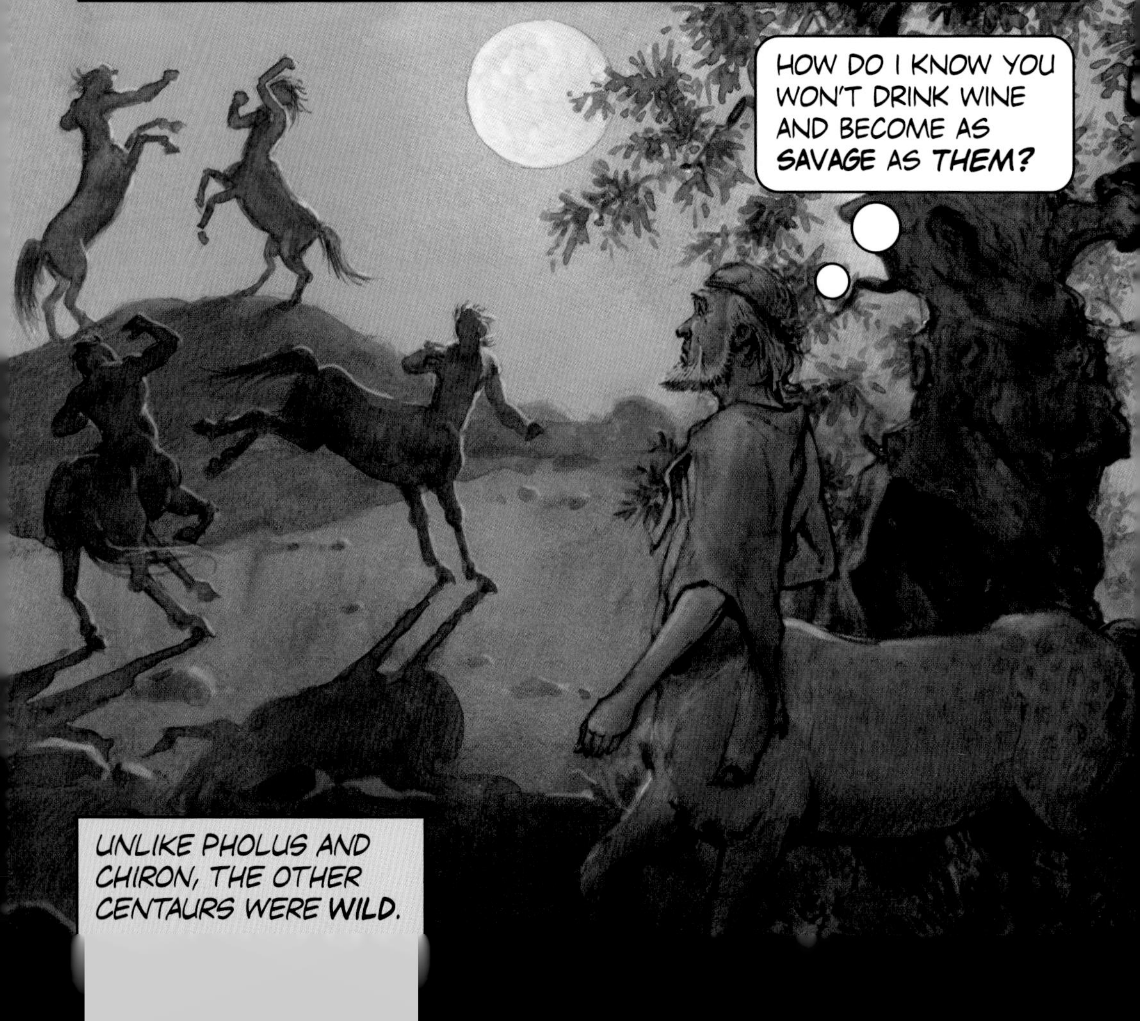
HOW DO I KNOW YOU WON'T DRINK WINE AND BECOME AS SAVAGE AS THEM?
UNLIKE PHOLUS AND CHIRON, THE OTHER CENTAURS WERE WILD.

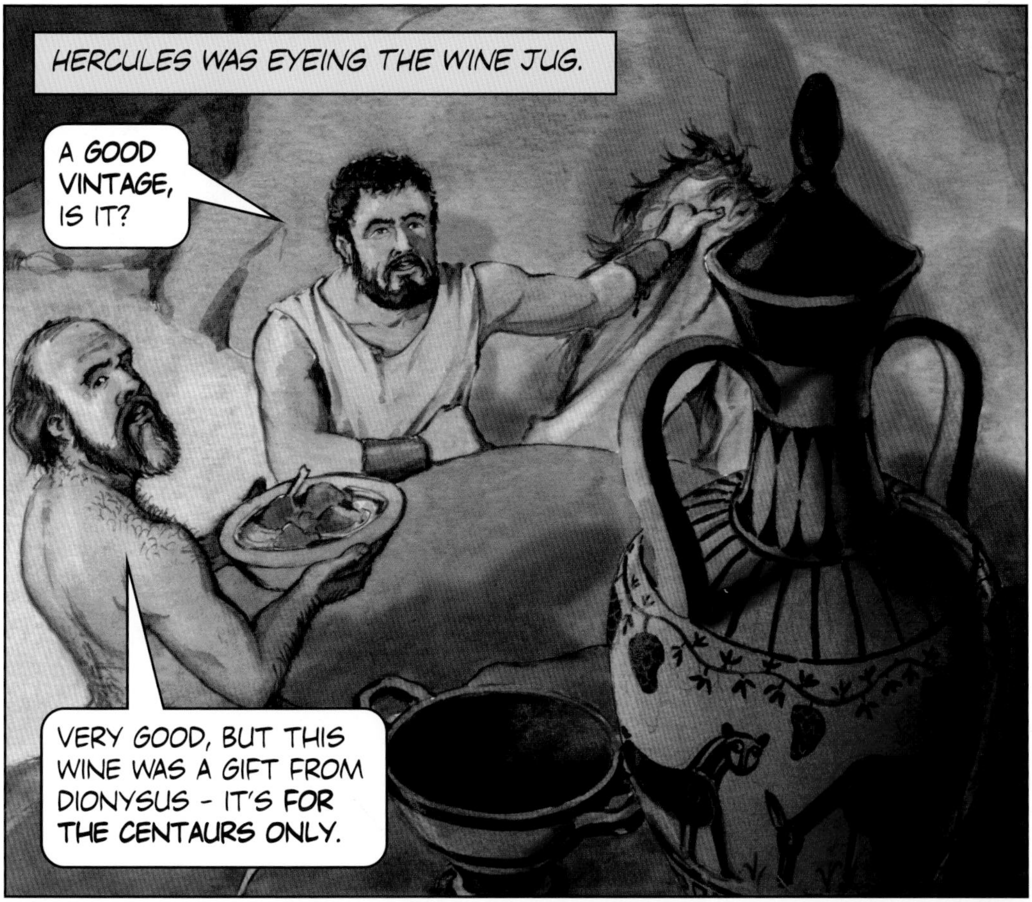
HERCULES WAS EYEING THE WINE JUG.
A GOOD VINTAGE, IS IT?
VERY GOOD, BUT THIS WINE WAS A GIFT FROM DIONYSUS - IT'S FOR THE CENTAURS ONLY.

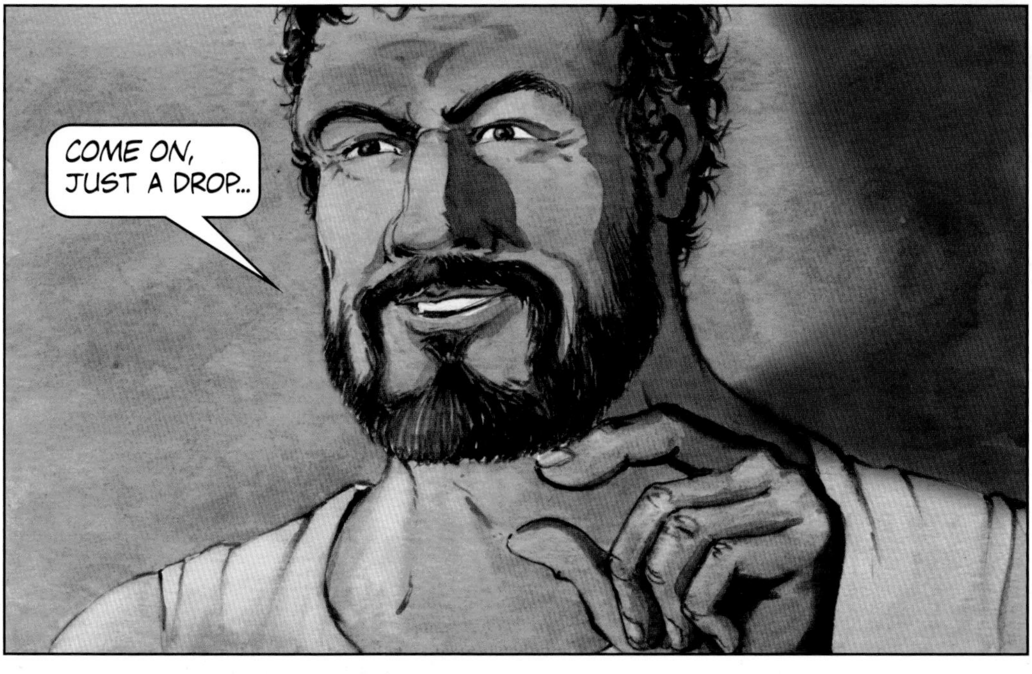
COME ON, JUST A DROP...

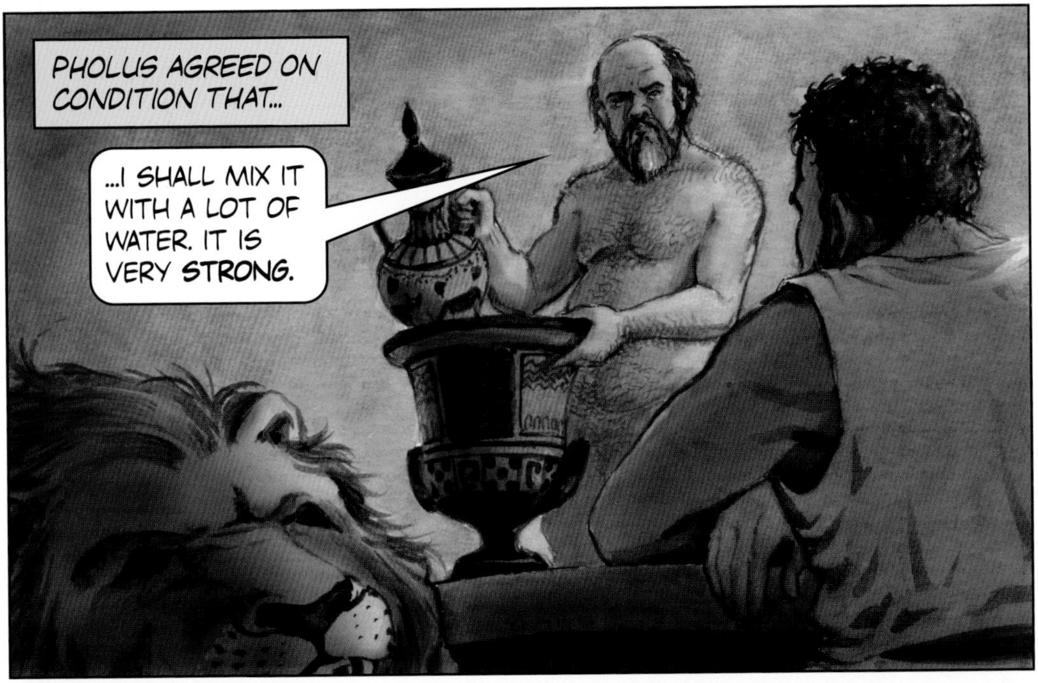
PHOLUS AGREED ON CONDITION THAT...
...I SHALL MIX IT WITH A LOT OF WATER. IT IS VERY **STRONG.**

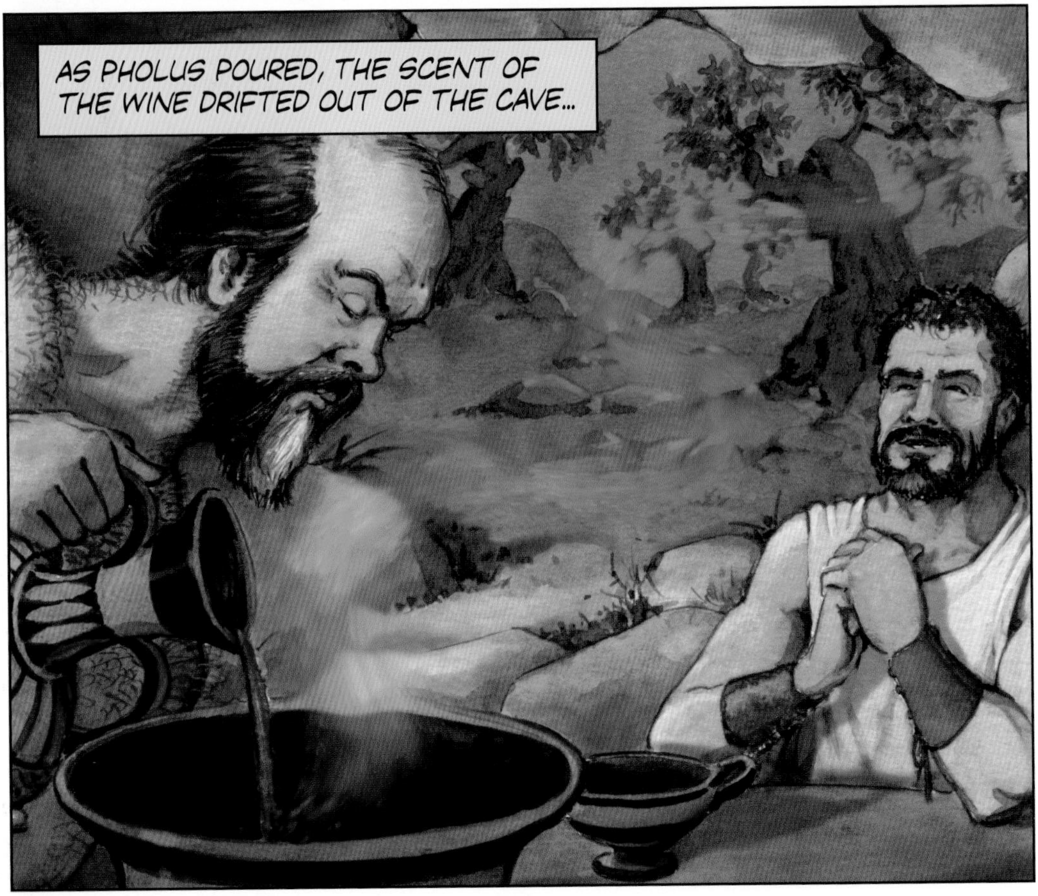
AS PHOLUS POURED, THE SCENT OF THE WINE DRIFTED OUT OF THE CAVE...

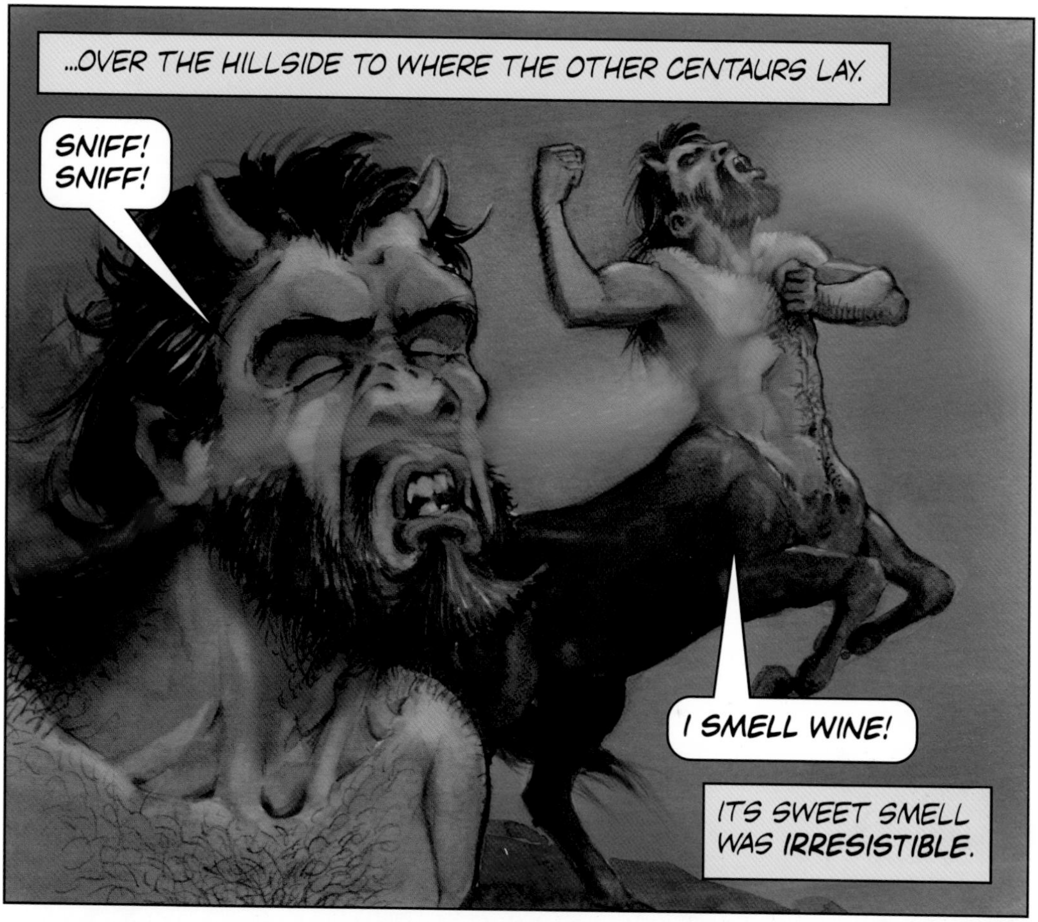
...OVER THE HILLSIDE TO WHERE THE OTHER CENTAURS LAY.
SNIFF! SNIFF!
I SMELL WINE!
ITS SWEET SMELL WAS **IRRESISTIBLE**.

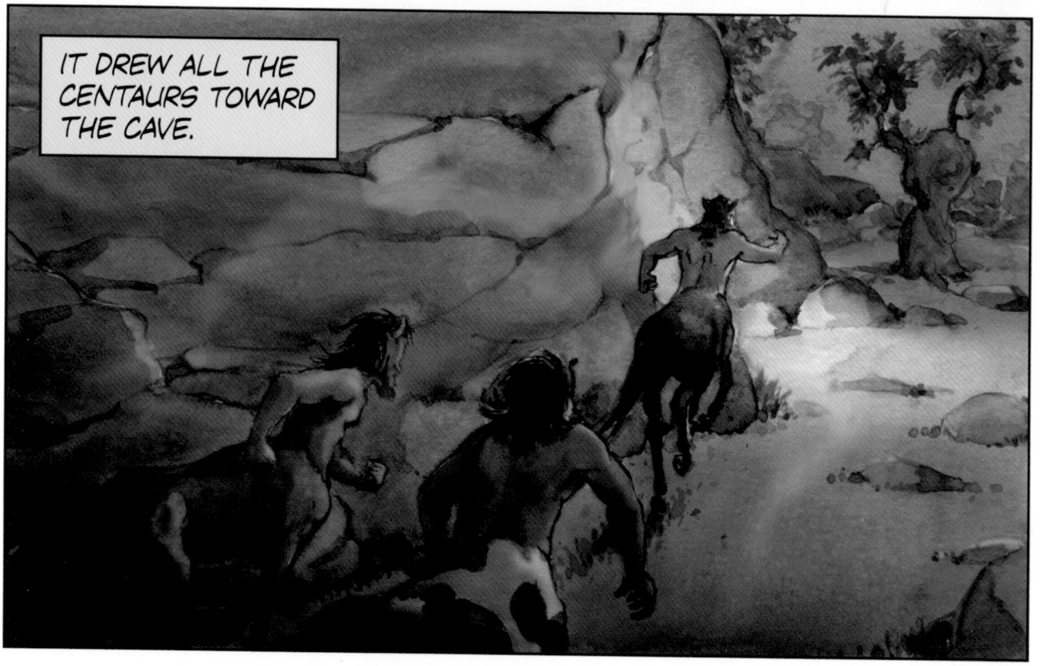
IT DREW ALL THE CENTAURS TOWARD THE CAVE.

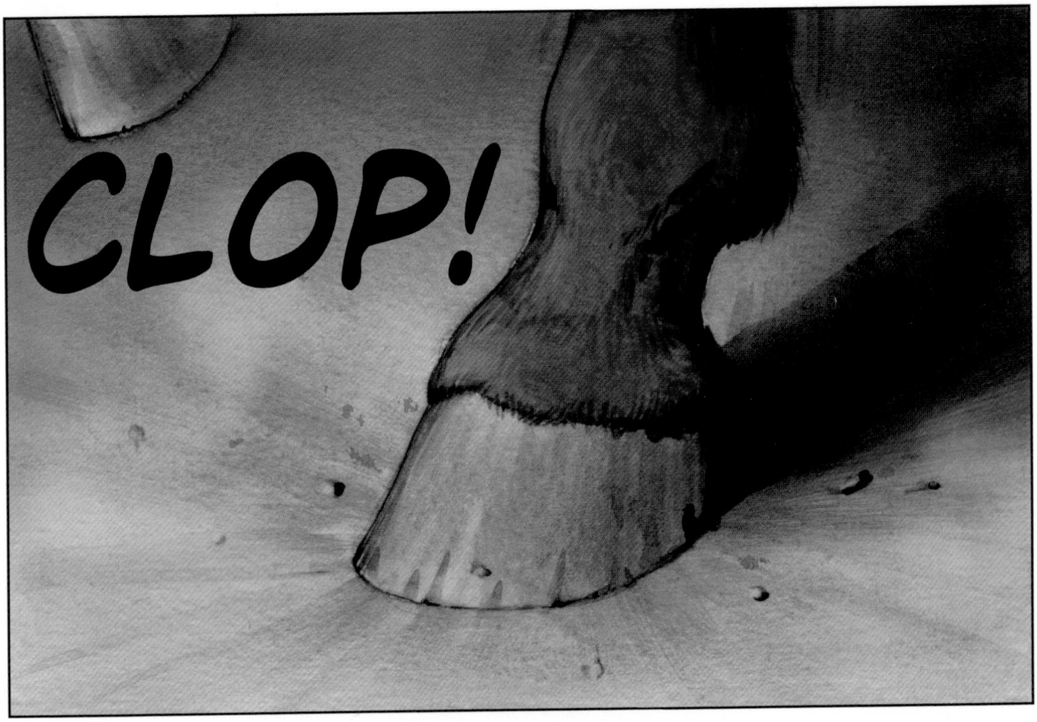
CLOP!

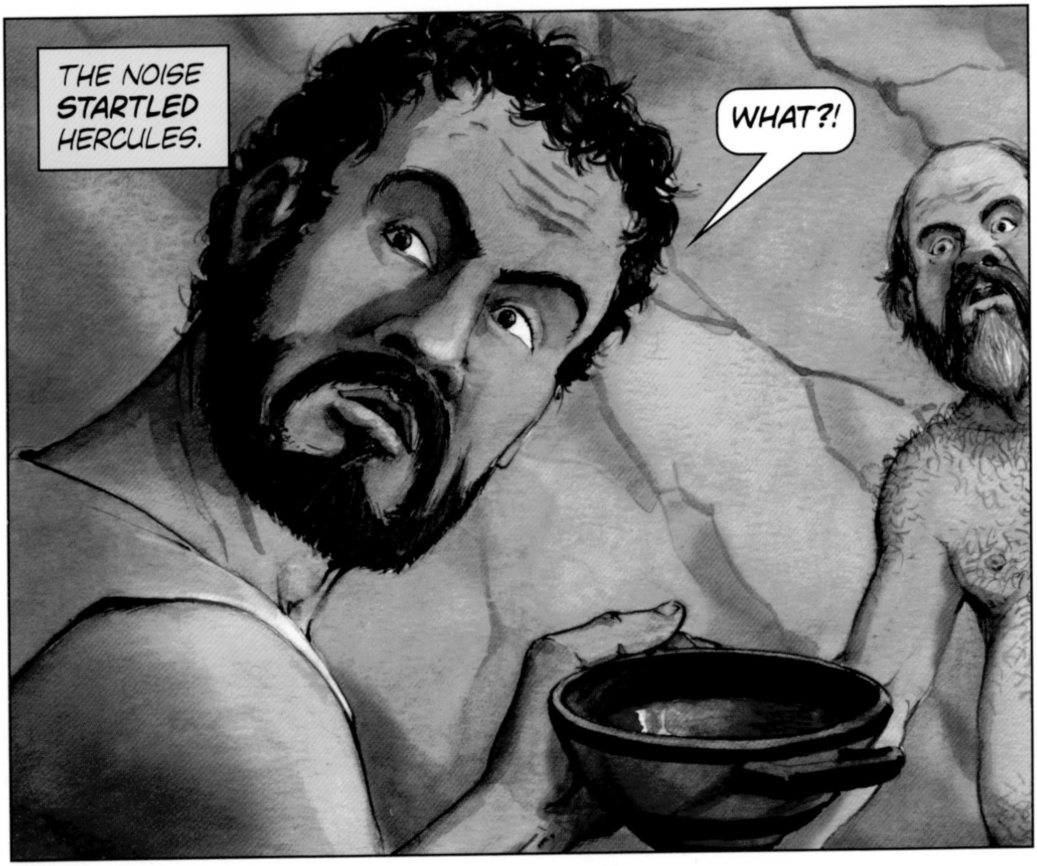
THE NOISE **STARTLED** HERCULES.
WHAT?!

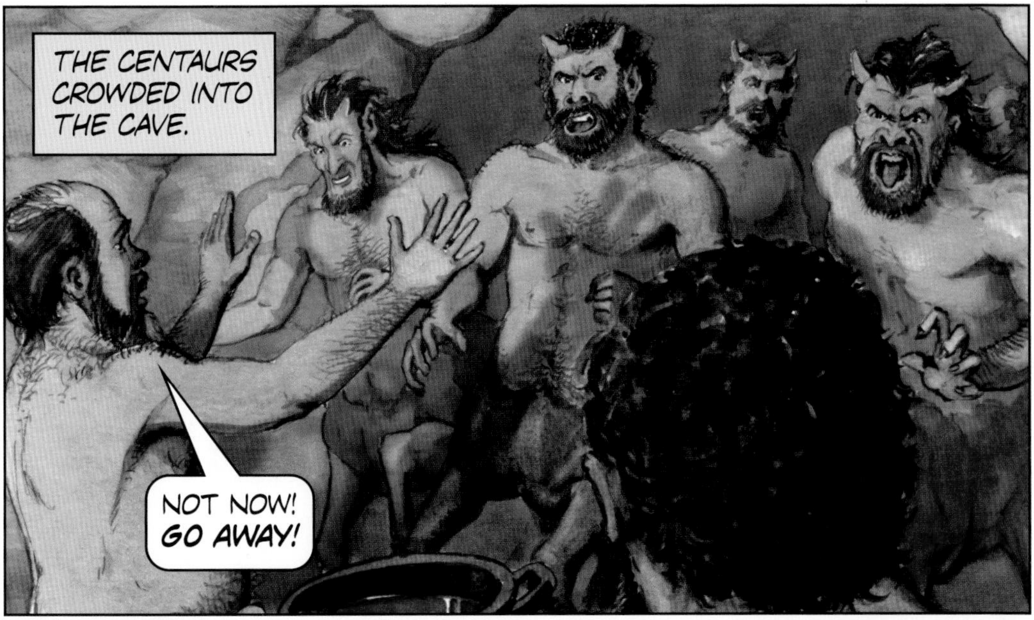
THE CENTAURS CROWDED INTO THE CAVE.
NOT NOW! GO AWAY!

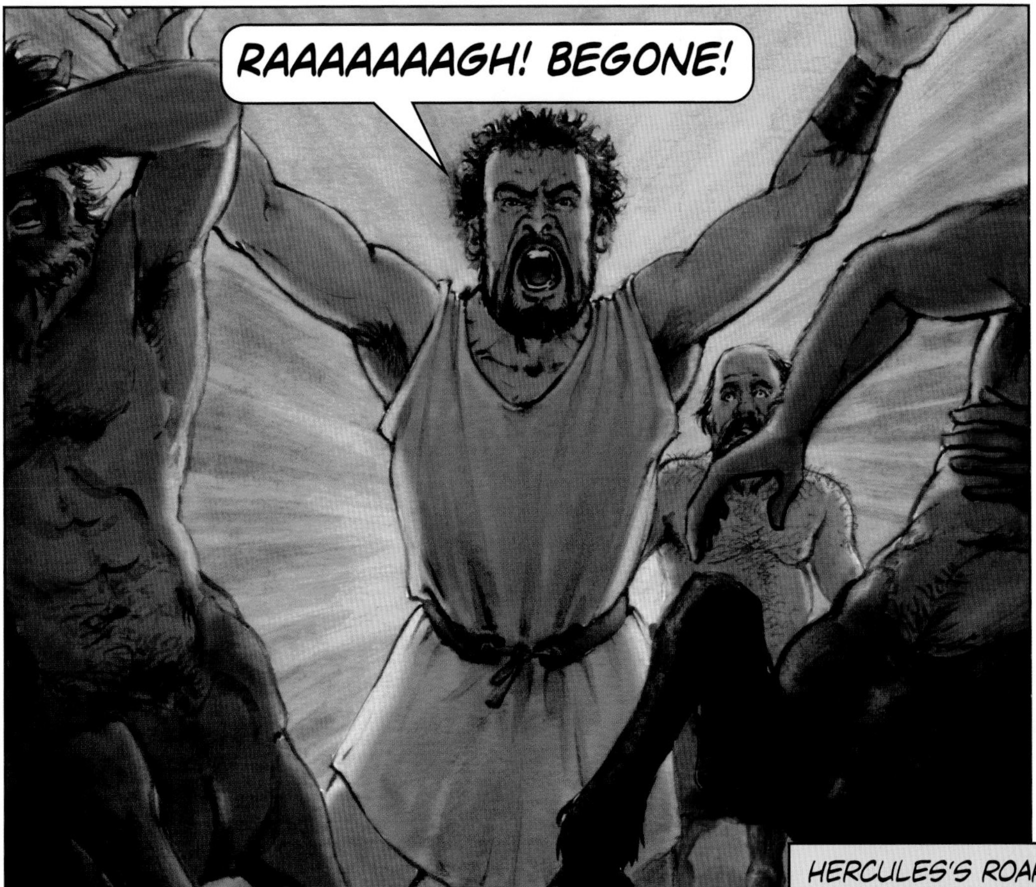
RAAAAAAAGH! BEGONE!
HERCULES'S ROAR SCATTERED THE CENTAURS.

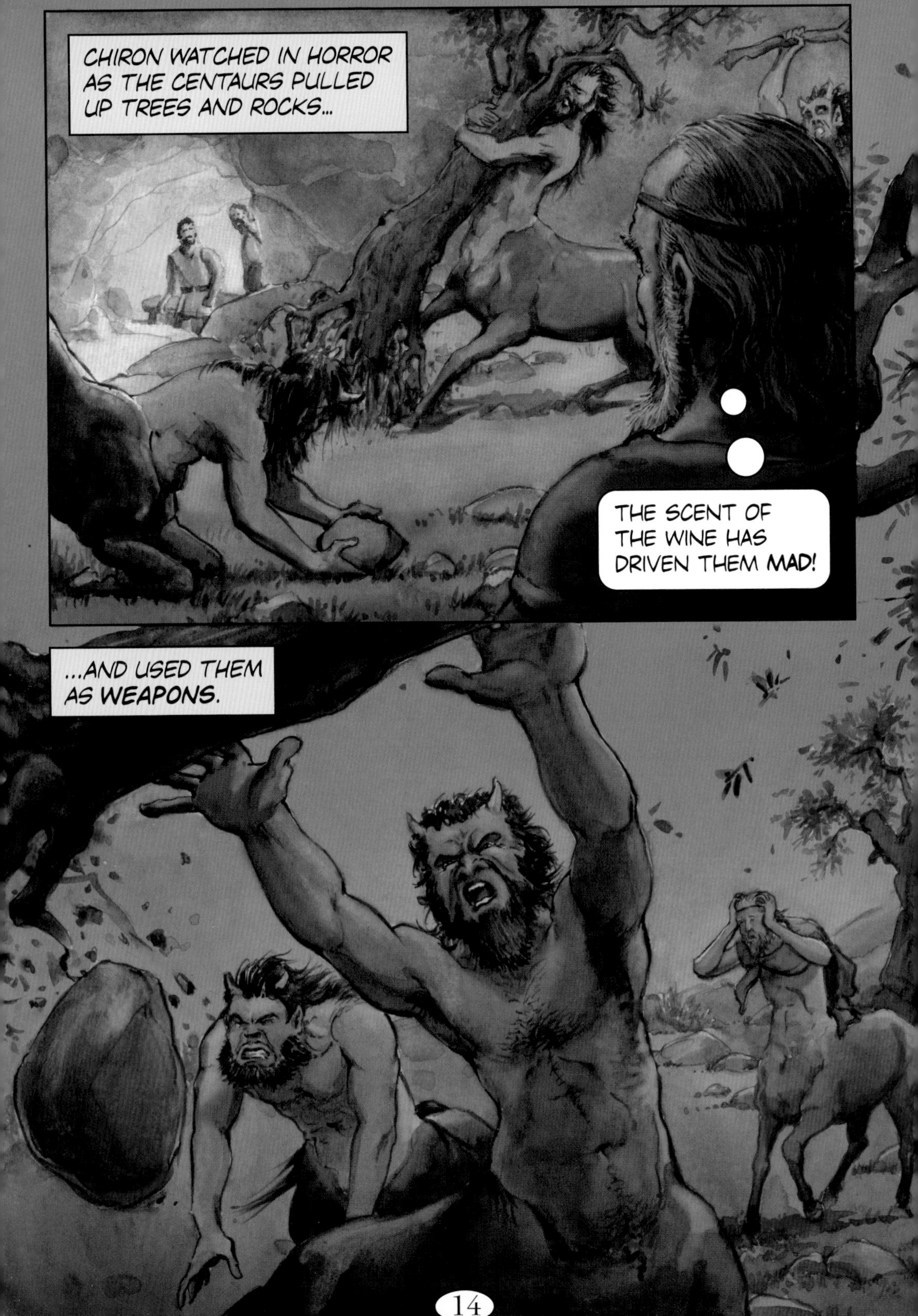
CHIRON WATCHED IN HORROR AS THE CENTAURS PULLED UP TREES AND ROCKS...
THE SCENT OF THE WINE HAS DRIVEN THEM MAD!
...AND USED THEM AS WEAPONS.

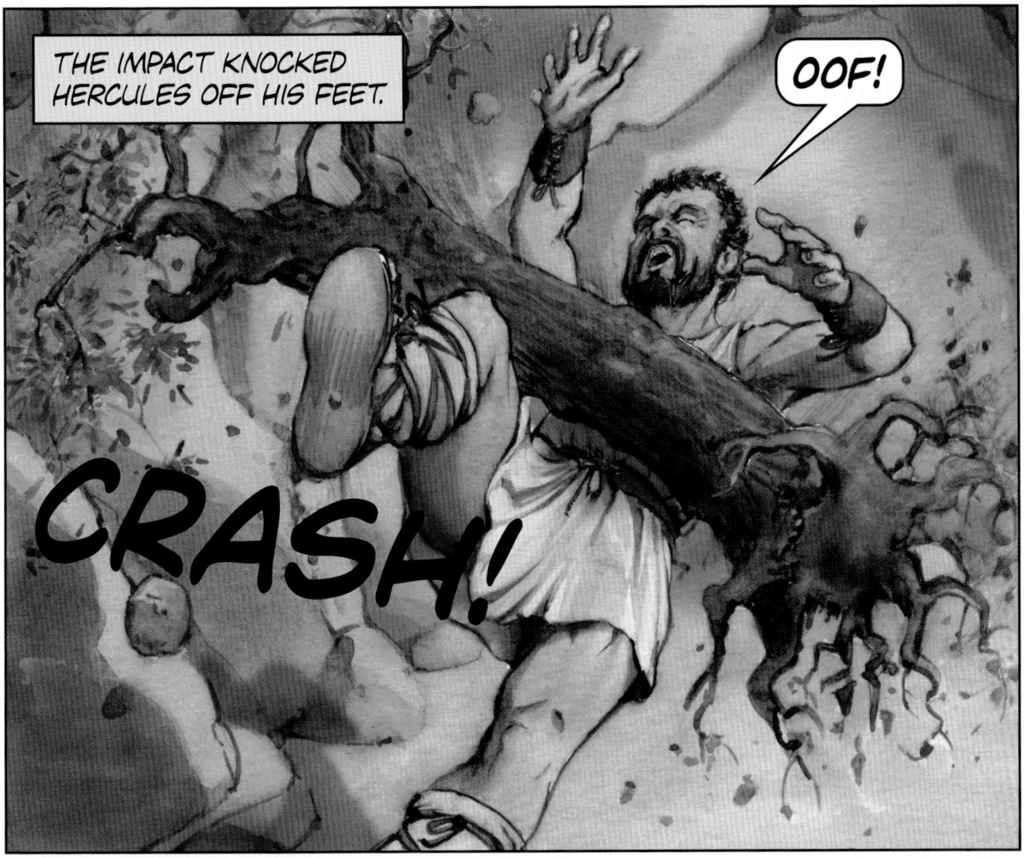
THE IMPACT KNOCKED HERCULES OFF HIS FEET.
OOF!
CRASH!

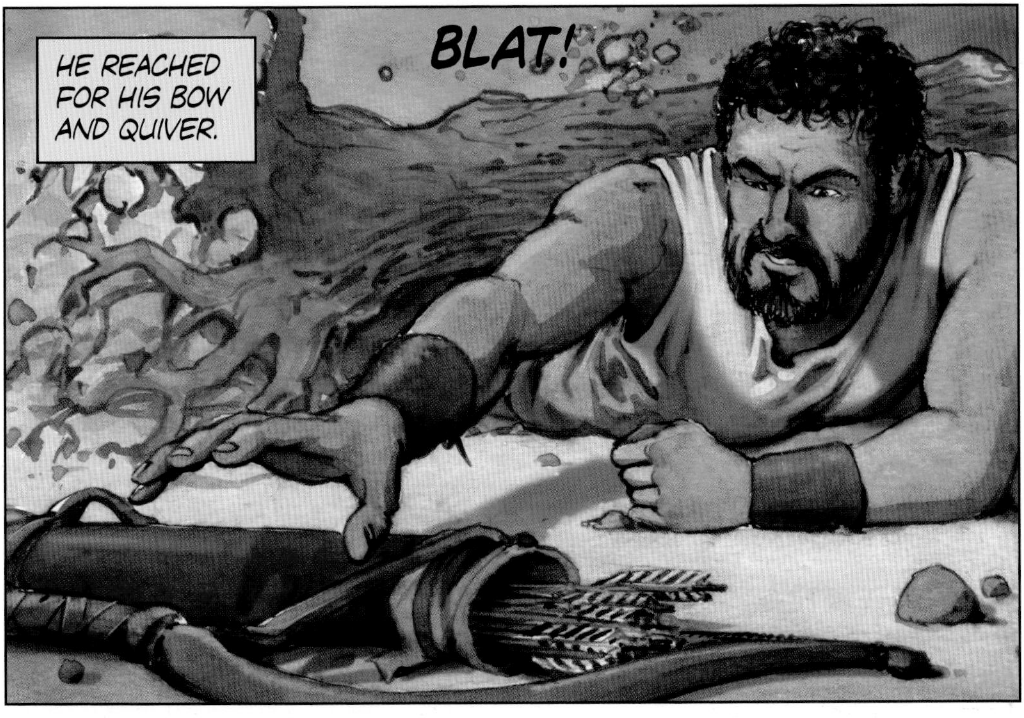
HE REACHED FOR HIS BOW AND QUIVER.
BLAT!

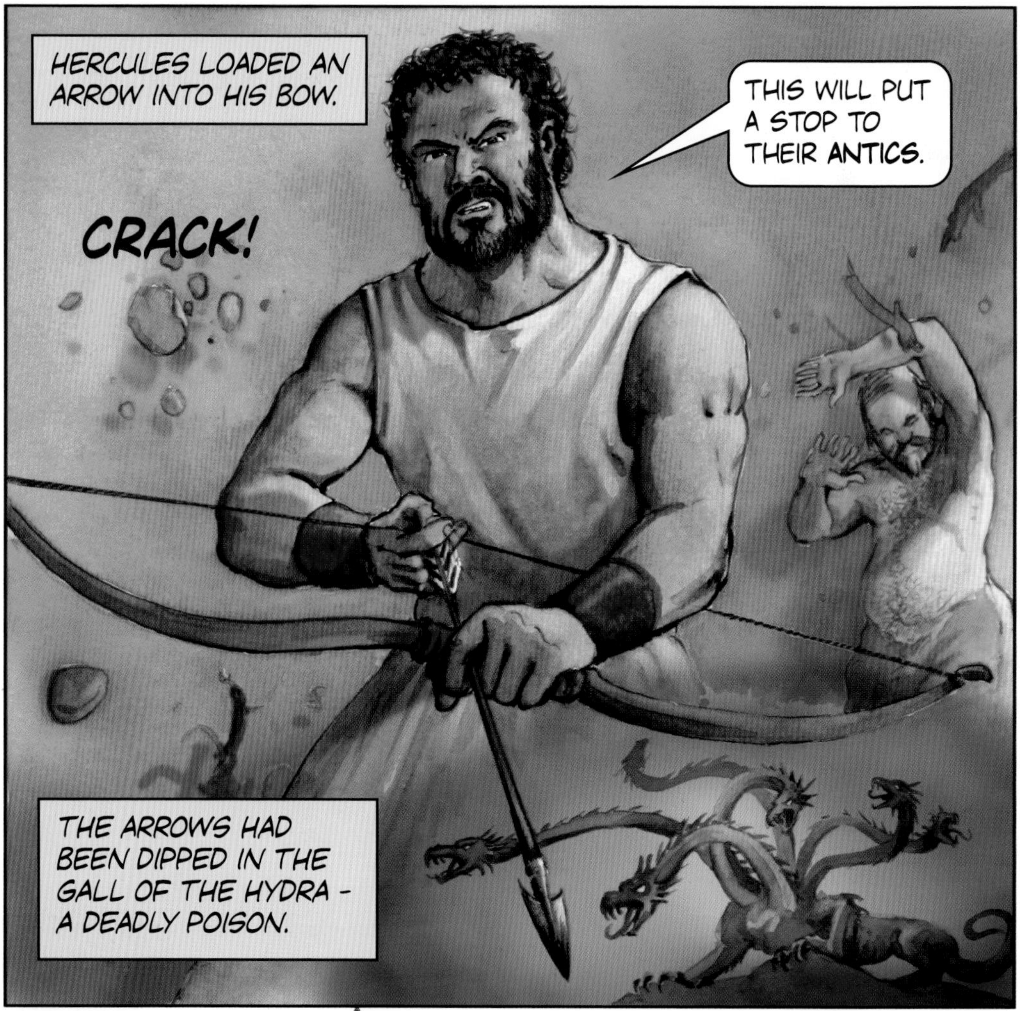
HERCULES LOADED AN ARROW INTO HIS BOW.
THIS WILL PUT A STOP TO THEIR ANTICS.
CRACK!
THE ARROWS HAD BEEN DIPPED IN THE GALL OF THE HYDRA - A DEADLY POISON.

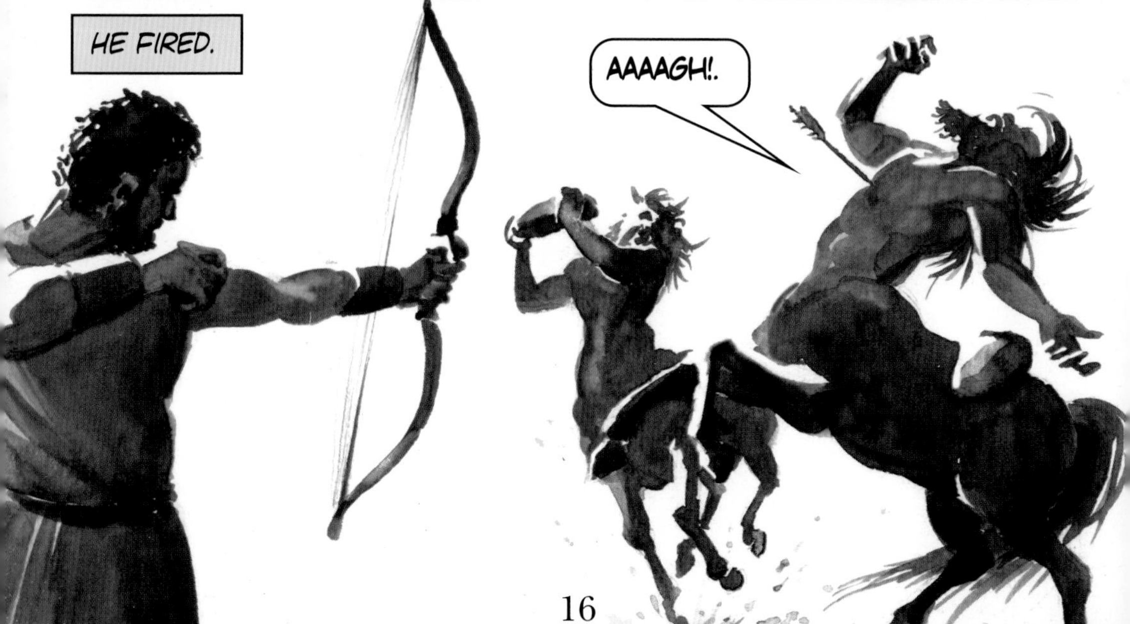
HE FIRED.
AAAAGH!.

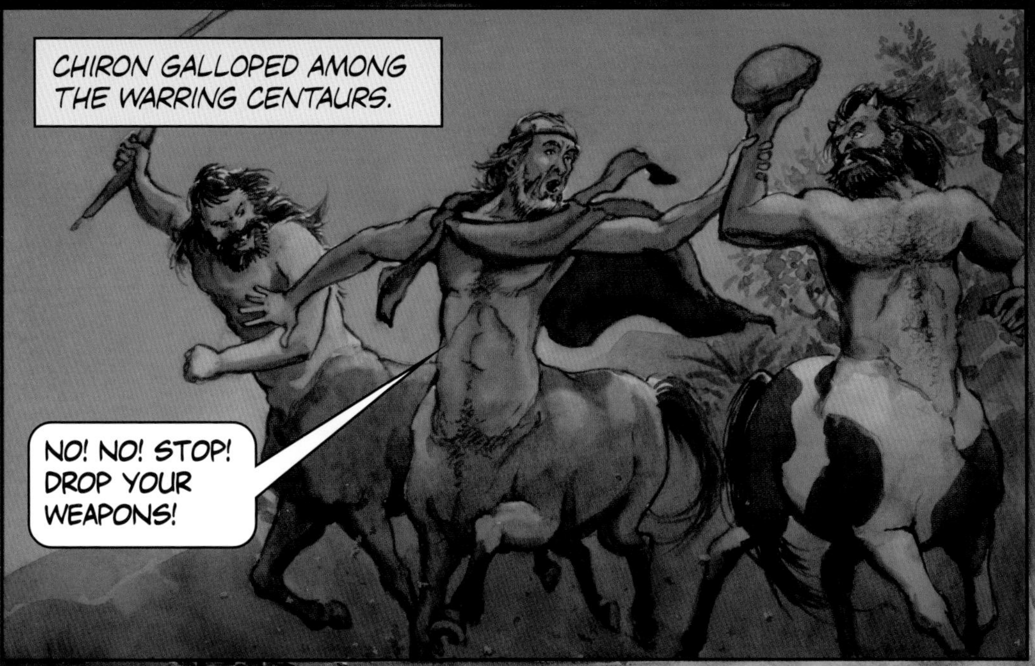
CHIRON GALLOPED AMONG THE WARRING CENTAURS.
NO! NO! STOP! DROP YOUR WEAPONS!

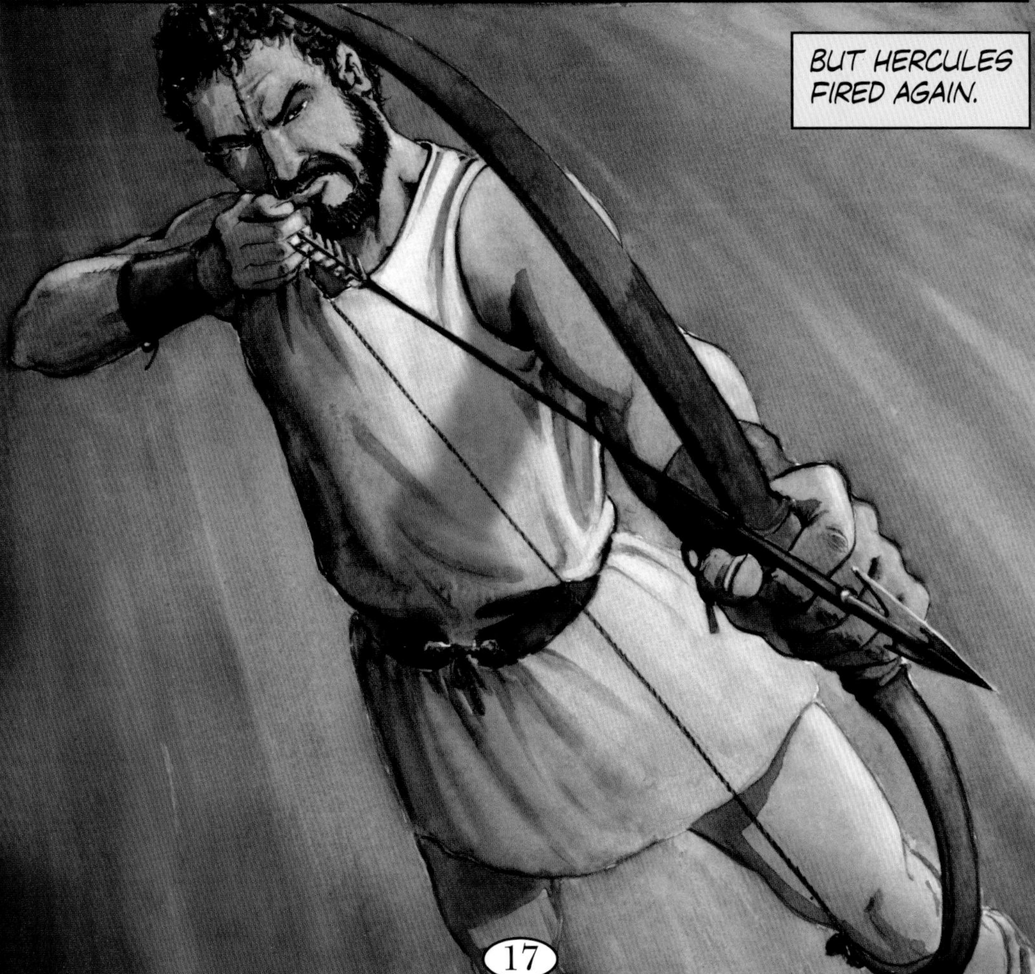
BUT HERCULES FIRED AGAIN.

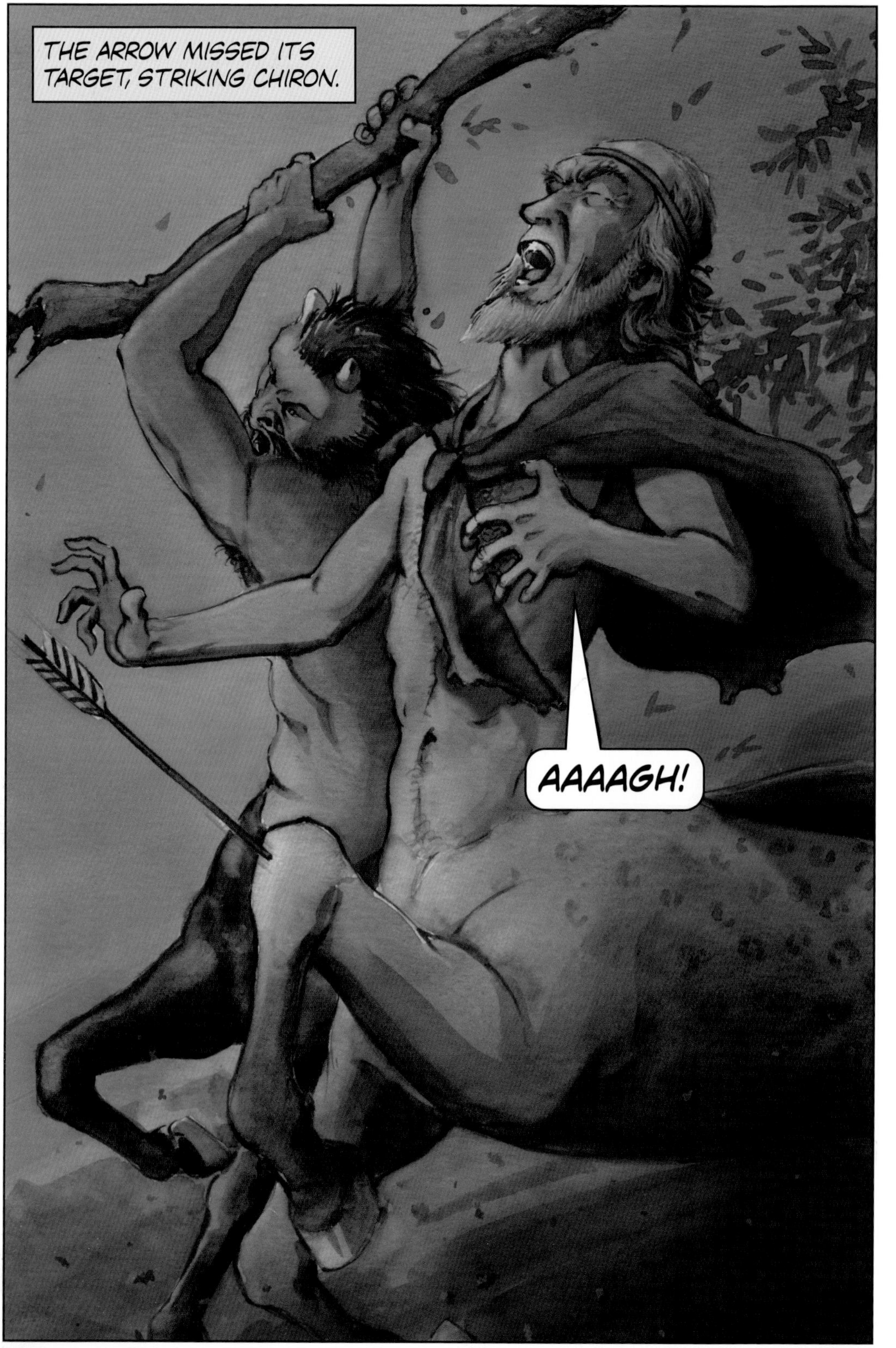
THE ARROW MISSED ITS TARGET, STRIKING CHIRON.
AAAAGH!

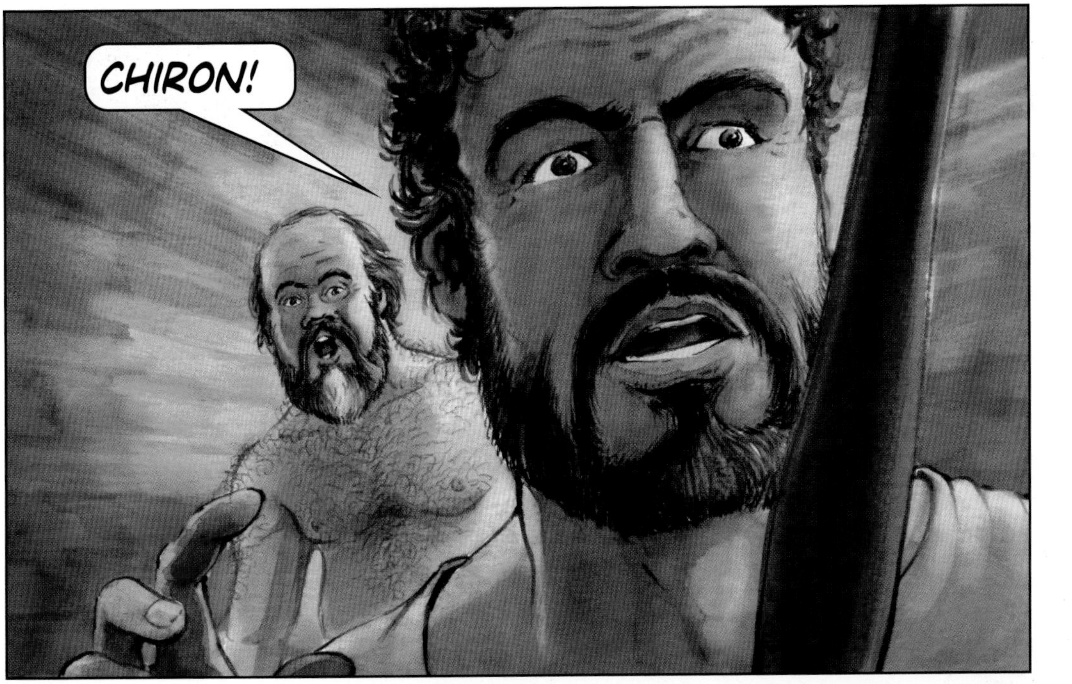
CHIRON!

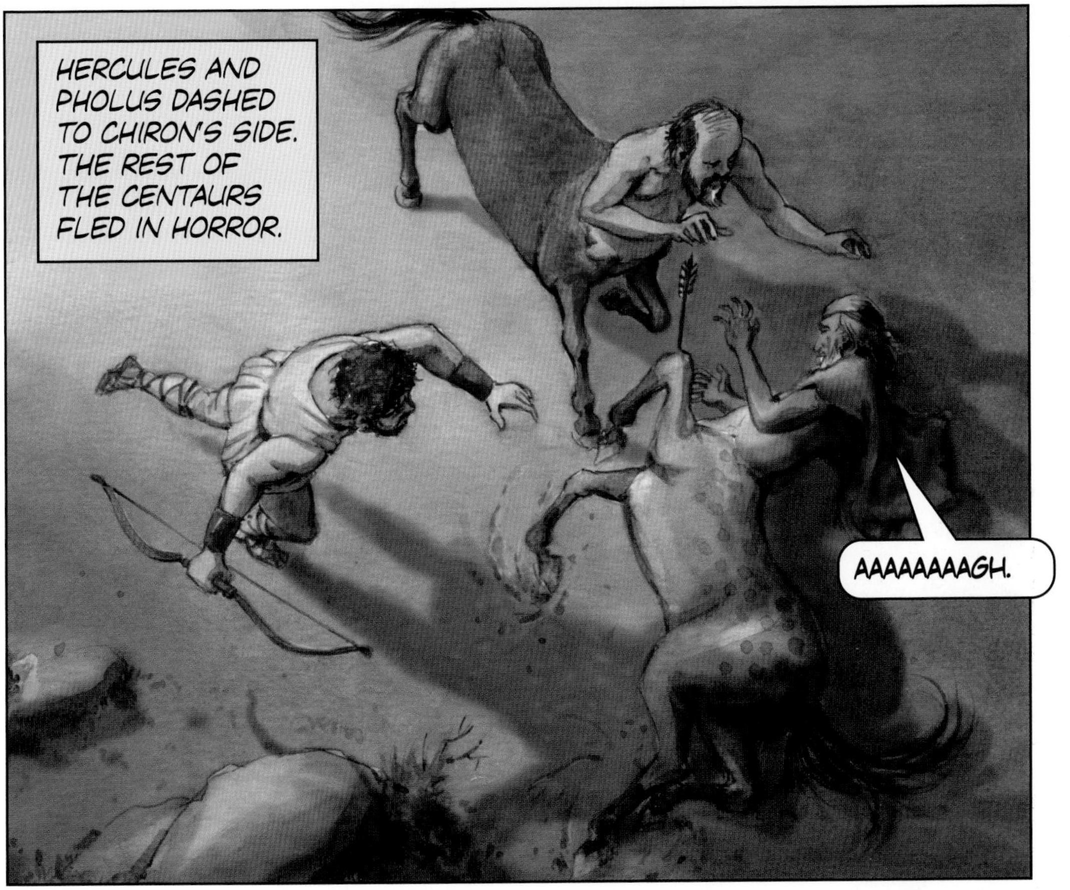
HERCULES AND PHOLUS DASHED TO CHIRON'S SIDE. THE REST OF THE CENTAURS FLED IN HORROR.
AAAAAAAAGH.

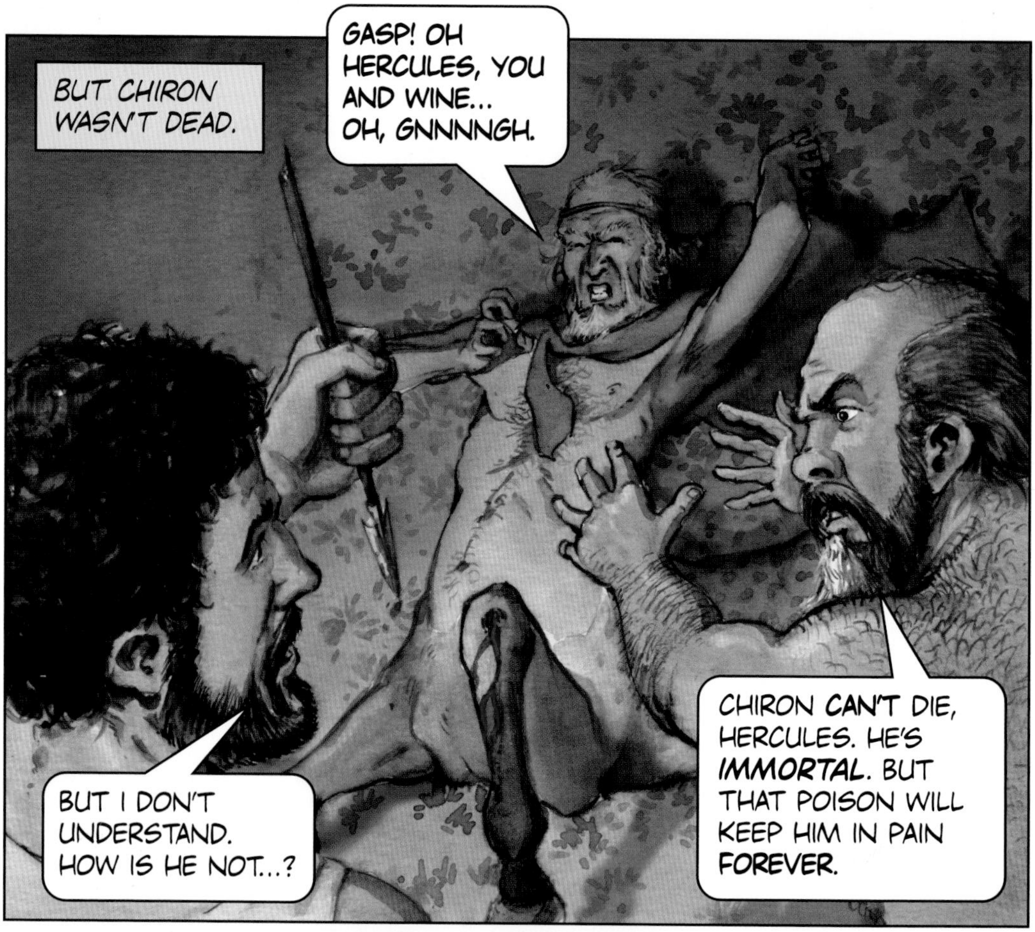
BUT CHIRON WASN'T DEAD.
GASP! OH HERCULES, YOU AND WINE... OH, GNNNNGH.
BUT I DON'T UNDERSTAND. HOW IS HE NOT...?
CHIRON CAN'T DIE, HERCULES. HE'S IMMORTAL. BUT THAT POISON WILL KEEP HIM IN PAIN FOREVER.

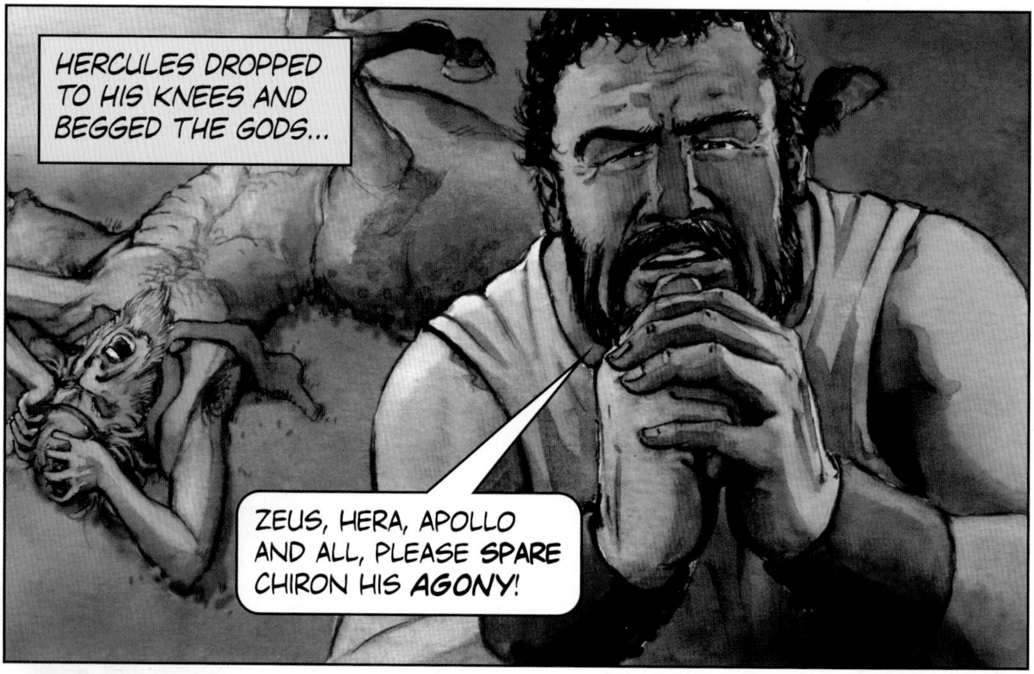
HERCULES DROPPED TO HIS KNEES AND BEGGED THE GODS...
ZEUS, HERA, APOLLO AND ALL, PLEASE SPARE CHIRON HIS AGONY!

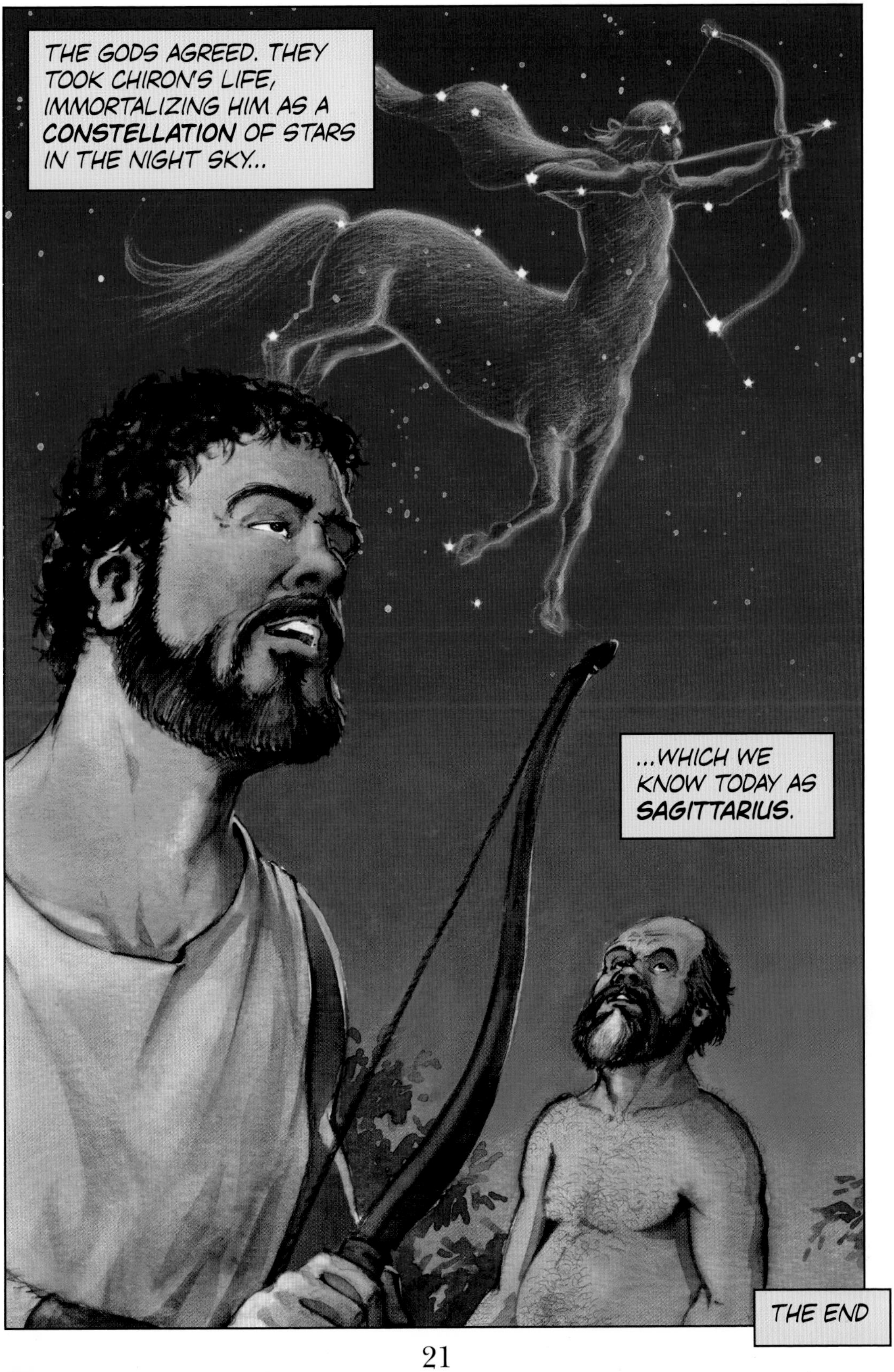
THE GODS AGREED. THEY TOOK CHIRON'S LIFE, IMMORTALIZING HIM AS A CONSTELLATION OF STARS IN THE NIGHT SKY...
...WHICH WE KNOW TODAY AS SAGITTARIUS.
THE END

OTHER CENTAUR TALES

There are many other mythical stories of centaurs' wild behavior, including, of course, the famed Centauromachy...

The Centauromachy

Ixion's son, Pirithous, king of the Lapiths, is marrying Hippodamia. Pirithous's cousins, the centaurs, are invited to the wedding feast. After drinking too much wine, Eurytus, the fiercest centaur, tries to carry off the bride. Tables are overturned. A brawl breaks out. Pirithous and his best friend, Theseus, jump in. Many Lapiths are killed, but it is the end for the centaurs as they flee, beaten and empty handed.

The Revenge of Nessus

Nessus the centaur, a survivor of the wedding feast, lived by the River Evenus working as ferryman. One day, Hercules arrived with his new wife, Deianeira. The river was flooded, so he asked

Hercules deals with Nessus on a Greek pot from the 5th century BC.

Nessus to carry her. Halfway across, Nessus decided to kidnap her instead. As Deianeira screamed, Hercules quickly shot Nessus through the heart with a poisoned arrow. When he was dying, Nessus gave Deianeira some of his blood, saying she could use it to keep Hercules true. When Hercules was leaving to go on a trip, she smeared the blood on his shirt. It was Nessus's revenge—the blood was still tainted with the arrow's poison, killing Hercules.

22

GLOSSARY

agony Intense pain or suffering.

antics Absurd actions or behavior.

brawl A noisy disagreement or fight.

constellation A group or arrangement of stars, given a
specific name.

eyeing Observing carefully and with interest.

ferryman Someone who uses a boat called a ferry to transport
people or things back and forth across a river or body
of water.

gall The bitter, green fluid known as bile that comes from parts
of an animal that are associated with the liver.

impact The force of a contact or collision.

quiver A case for carrying arrows, also the arrows themselves.

revel To celebrate, have noisy festivities, make merry.

savage Fierce, cruel, or uncivilized.

vintage The crop of grapes from a particular year.

INDEX